Praise for Highway Man:

Great short story with fully developed characters. I
look forward to anything Eden Winters decides to
publish and this one proves why.

> ~Mrs. Condit and Friends Read
> Books

The concert scene grabs you by the throat and shakes
you until you can't breathe but still feel like you're
dancing. ...Dayum but Eden Winters gets a lot into
fifteen thousand words.

> ~Cryselle's Bookshelf

The author packed such a wealth of life into such a
short story. Great Characters, great music, fantastic
stories.

> ~Feliz Faber

...the perfect short story—long enough to engage
and make it feel like a fully realized narrative, short
enough to read in one sitting and leave you wishing
for more Killy and Tex. A Small Gems Recommena-
tion.

> ~The Novel Approach

Other titles by Eden Winters:

The Angel of Thirteenth Street
Fallen Angel
Settling the Score
The Telling
Night Watch
The Wish
Duet
Naked Tales
Summer Boys
Tinsel and Frost
The Match Before Christmas
Fanning the Flames
A Lie I Can Live With
The Diversion series:
    Diversion
    Collusion
    Corruption
    Manipulation
    Redemption
    Reunion
    Suspicion

Highway Man

Eden Winters

ROCKY RIDGE BOOKS

Copyright © Eden Winters 2014
Cover art and interior layout by P.D. Singer
ISBN-13 978-1-62622-068-3

Published by:
Rocky Ridge Books
PO Box 6922
Broomfield, CO 80021
www.RockyRidgeBooks.com

First Edition 2011, Dreamspinner Press
Second Edition 2014, Rocky Ridge Books

For Eyre

Highway Man

Eden Winters

Highway Man

"But we need a lead guitar for more than one night, man! Our guy won't be back for two weeks."

Killian Desmond sighed, cell phone braced in one hand a few inches from his ear while half-eaten bacon and eggs congealed on a plate in front of him. The clicks and clacks of a busy diner competed with his call—an amazing feat, since the guy on the other end of the line shouted to be heard over a rock band in rehearsal.

In deep bass tones once described by a reporter as "smoky, with a hint of enter at your own risk," Killian replied, "And I done told you, one night's all I got. Take it or leave it. Gotta be in Denver the next morning." Yeah, he'd love the gig, but no way in hell was he sticking around any longer than one night. He frowned, both at the waitress offering more coffee and the caller refusing to understand plain English.

Ignoring his cold breakfast, he fired up a cigarette. Bluish smoke swirled toward the ceiling, to be batted away by the currents of an overhead fan. Nobody charged his table, demanding he put it out—despite the "No Smoking" signs plastered on the walls every few feet like grease-spattered pop art.

"What'd you say your name was again?" Killy's would-be employer's voice danced the razor's edge between cautious and paranoid.

"I didn't. I said I play lead guitar and do vocals, all you asked for in your ad. I can front or I can backup. Your choice."

1

"How long you been playing?"

"Long enough." The asshole didn't need to know about Mama bringing him and his older brother onstage starting at six and eight years old, hoping to squash junkie rumors by projecting a motherly image. The act hadn't worked, and the kiddies grew up on a tour bus, with pot, cocaine, and other drugs more readily available than bubble gum. Of course, trade a tour bus for cheap hotel rooms, drugs for booze and caffeine, and pot for tobacco, and you got *la vida del Papa*. Oh, yeah, and enough prescription painkillers to choke one of the broncs the man rode.

"I e-mailed you a lineup. You do know Trickster's songs, right?"

Trickster? Did he say "Trickster"? Oh shit. Killian hadn't read his e-mail yet or he wouldn't have taken this call. He swallowed hard around the solid lump of panic lodged in his throat. Trickster? A million friggin' bands out there, with a zillion freaking songs—why the fuck did the guy have to say Trickster? He came close to slamming the phone shut until recalling the four lonely twenties and handful of smaller bills in his billfold. Even the paycheck he'd collect later wouldn't tide him over indefinitely. Royalties simmered in a bank somewhere, but damned if he'd touch a cent until the vultures finished squabbling over who got what, and his mother's pitiful legacy languished in trust pending Killy's thirtieth birthday. *Money, money everywhere and not a dime to spend.*

"Yeah, I know their songs." Hell, he should. He'd written most of them.

"What'd you say your name was again?"

Oh, shit, here it goes. Maybe he should lie, hoping the leader of a band dedicated to his old songs never looked too closely at pictures on the CD cases. Then again, that one piece of info might guarantee him the job, but might also encourage the weekend warriors to beg him to stay, even if they did think him full of shit. No chance in hell of him staying.

"Killian Desmond," he replied, braced against the response he'd get. The novelty of a look-alike/sound-alike for a famous dead musician usually increased the take at whatever seedy bars he played. Using the name further boosted his appeal even though someone occasionally spat, "You ought to be ashamed of yourself, disrespecting that poor dead man!" If only they knew. However, in all his time filling in for bands wherever he could, this would be the first time he'd played Trickster's songs without Trickster. Even for a man who'd seen a lot in twenty-six years, this was too bizarre.

"Killian Desmond? Man, you're shitting me, right?" The guy paused, then snorted. "Good one. Who put you up to this? It was Ralph, wasn't it?"

"You ain't writing any IRS papers anyway. It don't matter if I *am* shitting you." Even though he wasn't. Killy pushed his greasy meal away, appetite vanishing along with his patience. "Look, you gonna hire me or not?"

The caller spoke words he'd heard a hundred times. "I wanna hear you sing."

Well, what could he expect? People weren't in the habit of hiring dead men, though a band missing a lead guitarist the day before a show couldn't afford to be choosy. He signaled the waitress that he'd be back, and stepped out into a day promising to be hot once the sun woke up properly. Rounding the back of the building, checking to ensure no one lurked around the corner, he began a deep, grumbling melody as familiar as his own hand, and as complicated as his life. He stopped after one verse.

It worked. "That was awesome!" his prospective band mate exclaimed, also something he'd heard hundreds of times. "I don't care what your real name is, if you play half as good as you sing, the job's yours. You almost sound like the real Killian Desmond! How much do you have to smoke a day to make your voice so gravelly?"

Killy ignored the question, "too many" being the honest answer. If the man didn't believe who he

3

was, so much the better. He'd learned the hard way: call himself Bill and people tended to speculate. If he called himself Killian Desmond and wielded a mean guitar, folks passed it off as a moneymaking scheme. And money was money. He'd pretend to be himself for one night for what they promised. The next day he'd go back to being another nameless drifter. "I'll be there tomorrow morning bright and early for a run through." They discussed particulars while Killy stopped by his ancient El Camino. He disconnected the call on a done deal and dug beneath a saddle and guitar case to extract a laptop left over from more prosperous days.

He reentered the diner, stubbing out his third smoke since he'd first arrived. Taking advantage of some local's unsecured Wi-Fi, he logged on to his favorite hookup site, both for gigs and bed partners, to cast a net over the area he'd be in for one night only—if he stayed that long.

M4M. Passing through. Good lkg, 26, NSA fun Friday nite. U host.

No need to reread his ad; he used pretty much the same message every time. "Good looking man seeking a no strings attached romp at some nameless guy's house." That ought to bring a few closet cases out with the promise of anonymous, discreet sex. He'd check tonight for hits. "Hits" brought a derisive snort. He'd had plenty of hits, once upon a time before the world went to shit.

He checked his e-mail, ignoring the bottom feeders with their hands out and his manager's, "Where the hell are you?" Fuck 'em. Fuck 'em all. The lineup could wait until later; it wasn't like he couldn't guess what songs he'd find. "Highway". Everyone always wanted to hear "Highway", Trickster's biggest hit.

He pulled out a tattered leather wallet and tossed a five and a few ones down on the table, eyeballing the liquid a hovering waitress kept pouring in lieu of coffee. The paint thinner in a cup wasn't worth finishing. Heartburn made a poor travel partner. No one so much as glanced at him as he strode out the door.

4

At one time he couldn't walk down a street without being mobbed by fans and paparazzi. Of course, at the height of his career, he couldn't have entered a rundown greasy spoon for breakfast without folks wanting pictures or autographs.

The seat of his El fit his ass like a glove. They'd bonded years ago. While not the most inconspicuous of vehicles, the aged relic didn't draw too much attention, even with the out-of-state plates. On the third attempt the engine fired up, and he added "new battery" to the growing list of things it'd need if he planned to keep on driving the darned thing. He only borrowed time. Without a major overall, the old boy would soon strand him on the roadside. BMWs, Corvettes, hell, even a Jaguar—he'd had them all in his time. And learned the hard way what really mattered. Cars sure as hell didn't. If only he'd figured out the truth years ago.

Old Man Tate, his most recent employer, met him in the driveway of the ramshackle farmhouse he'd called home for a few weeks. No, not home. The closest thing to home rode on wheels and God only knew where it was right now. Probably scattered across the country, a piece here and there in fans' living rooms. Killy squeezed his eyes shut and shook his head. Money-hungry assholes had literally ripped the twisted wreckage apart for souvenirs, to sell pieces of an expensive metal coffin online. There had to be a special place in Hell for those bastards.

"I sure wish you'd stay on with us. We got plenty more fence line to run," the rancher said, handing over a plain white envelope. "It's all there. Count it if you like."

"Nah, I trust you." Killy didn't, but the pile of bills bulging the envelope's sides paled against the need to believe in honest men.

"Sure you won't stay?"

"I appreciate the offer." And he did. "I gotta get on, though. Rodeo starts up this weekend." Not to mention a month in one place made Killy's skin crawl to be back on the move.

He stopped a few miles down the road, giving in to curiosity about the contents of the envelope. His lips turned up on one side in a semi-smile of satisfaction, causing the deep scar at the edge of his mouth to pull. Old Man Tate was honest, after all. Killian tucked the money away into his laptop case.

The drive through Montana proved uneventful, miles and miles of unbroken I-90. "Gonna take the scenic route next time," he promised himself, a promise usually broken for the sake of time. It seemed a man with no steady job should have plenty of the damned stuff, but he fell short all too often.

Under a camper shell in the back of the El Camino rode all his worldly possessions, except for his laptop, saddle, and guitar, crammed together on the passenger seat and on the floorboard. He lit a cigarette. It wasn't a crutch to postpone the inevitable, not at all. When his cigarette burned to embers, he lit another from its dying corpse.

"Fuck it!" He tossed the half-smoked coffin nail out the window and blew out a nicotine-laced breath. Had he downed a Prozac today? Yesterday? A little rooting underneath his saddle produced a brown container. He shook the bottle. Damn, only one more pill. He'd have to get a refill soon, and filling 'scripts was a sure-fire tracking tool for those he wanted to avoid. Well, no help for that. Plenty of folks at the rodeo supplied what he needed, and off the grid. Last thing before leaving Denver, he'd hit a Mom and Pop pharmacy. By the time anyone pinpointed his location, he'd be long gone.

He slung the bottle aside. Stretching to reach into the glove compartment while driving, he fumbled out a CD and flipped the case over to hide the image of the smiling young men on the cover. All dead now, according to the media.

That whole dying thing made great public relations. If only his manager had thought of killing off a few band members sooner. CD sales soared through

the roof following the crash. A disc of previously unre-
leased works, hastily thrown together to capitalize on
the band's name hijacking headlines, went multi-plat-
inum and won a Grammy. Whose wall did it hang on?

He slid the shiny silver disc into the CD player.
Time to knock some rust off the old vocal chords. A
hard-as-diamonds guitar riff fired from the speakers.
His fingers itched to play for real, bad memories not-
withstanding. Soon enough, soon enough. *One, two,
three, four...* Killy joined his voice to the music, beating time against the steering wheel.

His heart hammered and his hands grew sweaty
when the first verse ended and the chorus began, her-
alding a voice that still echoed in his head after three
long years. His brother's gorgeous tenor wrapped
around Killy's "dragging the riverbed" growl, harmo-
nizing like they'd sung together for years. They had.
Nearly from birth. Now Killy sang alone, Elliot's voice
silenced forever.

Dang, but the sun was bright. Made his vision
blurry. He blinked against the sting, swallowing
around the lump in his throat created by singing with
himself and three of the dearly departed. Dearly Departed would have been a much better name for their
band than Trickster, a moniker conceived from Elliot's
obsession with Norse gods back in their teens.

The song faded and another began. Killy hit the
"forward" button—hard. No way could he torture himself with hearing his brother and that jackass drummer, Rob, wailing about true love, like Rob even knew
what love meant. Or Elliot ever got the chance to learn.

The CD played several times through before Killy
stopped for a burger and to fill up the El. Time to call
it a day. He located a flea-bag motel near the interstate
offering a free Internet connection. A truck stop next
door might be the perfect place to solve other cravings;
he'd keep it in mind. Since losing his virginity in the
sleeper cab of a Peterbilt while Mama snorted coke in
the bus, he'd come to see truck stops as mini-marts for

sexual snacks. Barn stalls and closeted cowboys served the purpose during summers spent with Papa.

Faces and names—if he'd ever known them—created one big blur of memories, too many to count. And no reason to. He'd gotten what he'd wanted, and so had they. Everyone walked away happy. Unlike Elliot, Killy didn't write songs about fantasies like love. He stuck with the real world: sex and drugs and endless highways. And rock and roll. Elliot the dreamer. Killy the realist. "Life sucks," he'd often told his brother. "Whoever survives longest is the winner."

Sometimes winning and losing traveled hand-in-hand.

Killy hauled his stuff into a dingy room and settled his laptop on a rickety desk to search for gold. First he checked the Triksterz line-up (he huffed and rolled his eyes at the cover band's name), approving some choices, wondering what the hell they were thinking with others. He replied, "I'm afraid I don't know Highway." He'd play any other song from his band's three albums, except "Highway". No way, no how.

Next, he checked his posting. His ad paid off with five responses—two from spambots and one from a right-winger.

You're going to hell, you damned pervert!

Tell him something he didn't know.

Two other messages left.

Bi-male, 35, wife out of town, wants to get fucked. Safe or BB, whatever.

Oh, hell no. Killy's standards didn't allow fucking the stupid. The second response was a little more to his liking.

Gay male. 22. Versatile. Can host for NSA, possibly more.

Infinitely better, even if "possibly more" wasn't an option. The guy included a nude picture, taken from the neck down. Not bad, not bad at all. Not a gym rat, though; those long, lean muscles looked to be earned the hard way. His erection jutted proud and tall against a background of dark treasure trail. The face didn't really matter with a body like a god. Yes, very nice indeed. Killy dashed off a quick response.

Parking lot, Rarin' Stallion, 11 pm. '68 Red El Camino. Come early, watch show. Nothing stoked fires hotter than bringing out a potential fuck's inner groupie.

With something promising waiting a little more than twenty-four hours away, no need to go prowling the truck stop for some fat, balding trucker with a beer gut and a taste for cock. Instead, Killian turned in early. He might need the rest.

The next day he entered Wyoming at dawn, heading for a mid-sized town he'd never seen before. Strike one more off the list of places he'd been to and probably wouldn't do again. A deserted, early-morning side street presented an eerie blast from the past. The Rarin' Stallion bore a striking resemblance to Tails, the second-rate club where his and Elliot's hastily thrown together band had played their first gig without Mama, and where they'd found Rob, the psychopath drummer who'd blown their world apart.

What a dive. He'd bet good money that the run-down club came complete with a cheap '70s disco ball.

No one greeted him when he sauntered through the front door, guitar case slung over one shoulder. The scent of stale beer and greasy French fries made the three cups of coffee in his stomach roll.

Decent sized dance area, bar located to the back, smallish but workable stage, and fuck it all, a disco ball. He'd played better venues, and he'd played worse.

A bad rendition of Trickster's "Four on the Floor" assaulted his ears.

The men onstage didn't look much like a rock band—they'd appear more at home sucking back brews in a fishing boat, with their John Deere ball caps and T-shirts touting everything from country music to the NFL.

And the lead singer better not quit his day job.

The keyboardist hit a sour note and they all stopped to stare at Killy.

"Damn! You'd even look like Killian Desmond if you'd let your hair grow longer and add some blue streaks. And if you didn't have that scar across your face." The lead singer and manager for Triksterz scrutinized him with squinted eyes. If the smarmy little toad were green he'd look right at home catching flies with his tongue. *Bet no one's ever tossed panties and hotel keys on the stage at your ugly ass.*

Killian ran his hand over his scrubby, dirty-blond buzz cut, and trailed his fingers lower across the ragged reminder of the night spent in hell. A deep gash marred his right cheek, permanently puckering the corner of his mouth. "I hear that all the time." *Because it's true,* went unsaid.

The homely little front man made introductions all around, winking when presenting Killy as "Killian Desmond."

The guys smiled, laughing and nodding at the joke, all except for a tall, cool drink of water with blue-black hair and brown eyes. Running an assessing gaze up and down Killian's body, the bass player switched the neck of his guitar to his left hand and extended his right. *Well, whattya know? A left handed bassist, just like Elli—* Killian stopped the memory on a dime. He'd gotten good at turning his brain off on command.

"Mike Rose. I'm fillin' in too," the living, breathing bass player said, in an ice-melting Texas drawl. Like Killy would remember the name a split second later. Names were for people he'd know longer than a day. He dubbed the guy "Texas." A pity, though. The man exuded sex appeal. No doubt he had women and men both waiting around after shows, just hoping to be the night's lucky pick.

Highway Man

They shook hands, Killy taking in Texas' knowing smirk. So, out of four members of a Trickster tribute band, one shared a common interest with the real deal: a definite liking for the male gender. The handshake continued longer than necessary. Locking gazes, they performed a silent, more intimate introduction, one best continued later in private. Maybe Killy ought to ditch tonight's faceless mystery date for this sure thing.

Formalities over, he released his guitar from its holding cell, plugged into an amp, tuned up a bit, then launched into one of the riffs that had made him famous. The other musicians hesitated a moment, staring at him in with their mouths hanging open. "Well, what are you waiting for?" from the leader urged them to action. "Let's try 'Overkill'." Killy started in on the lead vocals. The strutting little peacock shot him an evil glare. *Oh shit. Did he mean....*

Fuck if he didn't. When the chorus started, "I'm the lead singer, dammit" made summoning motions with his hand for Killy to join the duet. For the first time in his life, Killy sang Elliot's part, though much lower pitched since no way in hell could he ever hope to match his brother's vocal range.Elliot sang; Killian growled—at least according to the critics. Killy hadn't sung harmony even while writing the blamed song, always commanding the melody. *Turn it off, Killy. Don't think, don't feel...* Damn, but he needed more Prozac.

Why the fucking hell did he torture himself like this? Oh yeah. Green stuff to buy food and gas. That's why.

"Now let's do 'Highway'," the front man said after the first song faded.

Fuck. "Don't know it," Killy snapped.

"You what? You said you knew Trickster's music."

"I do. Just not 'Highway'." *No way in hell, no way in hell...*

"Well, fuck." The guy glowered. Let him sulk.

The band themselves weren't half bad. Not as good as Trickster, but they didn't suck completely. Too bad the lead singer couldn't carry a tune in a bucket.

11

The keyboardist wasn't star quality, but decent for a bar band. The drummer had damn well better improve by tonight. The bassist? He'd made a wrong turn somewhere to wind up with these losers. The man could play. Sing too.

They wrapped up rehearsal, the leader satisfied to have found "a last minute replacement that won't make us sound too bad." If they weren't paying, Killian would have walked.

It's just for tonight. Why did he ever answer that ad?

And why didn't he ask more questions when the arrogant prick said, "We're a tribute band, almost as good as the real thing." *Just play the gig, take the money, and run.*

"Be back here at eight," the commandant of Triksterz ordered as the band made their way outside. "We're on at nine, off at eleven."

As if Killy didn't already know, having been told fourteen times already during rehearsal. The rest of the band crawled into their vehicles, leaving him alone in the parking lot. Or rather, he thought he was alone until a libido-stroking drawl sounded behind him. "It's a bit early, Mr. Red El Camino in the Rarin' Stallion parking lot, but I've never really lived my life on much of a schedule anyhow."

Killy turned around, and fell into a pair of mahogany-colored eyes; a dark crow's wing of an eyebrow cocked a question. Oh, damn. He pictured the strapping body he'd seen on the Internet. His cock stiffened in his jeans. Oh yeah. They sure knew how to grow them in Texas.

He lit a cigarette and popped the top on the bottle of beer he'd sneaked from behind the bar. Didn't that just beat all? Nine hours to kill, and he'd just been offered the perfect way to do them in. What a coincidence, bumping into his after work appointment early.

"I don't do one night stands," Killian said, to get things out in the open from the get-go. Saved him awkward moments later. He took a long pull of his brew, letting the ice-cold beverage clear the dryness from his throat.

He eyed Tex up and down, measuring him for size. Yes, a nice, comfortable armful, this one: all rugged masculinity, wrapped in faded jeans and a worn chambray work shirt. The growth of beard and moustache neatly trimmed around his mouth checked off an item on Killy's "can't resist" list.

The catch of the day smiled, showing even, white teeth, and tilted his Stetson back with the bottle of Bud fused to his hand. Seemed Killy wasn't the only one who'd done a little pilfering in the bar. "You don't strike me as the long-term type, and that's not what your ad said."

Killy gulped from his beer again. "No, not long-term and not short-term either. I just don't stick around the whole night, is all."

His comment brought the most genuine laugh Killy'd heard in a long, long time. He'd have been tempted to join in if his confession wasn't the God's honest truth instead of a joke.

"Where've you got to go that's so all-fired important?"

"Nowhere, anywhere." No matter how hard he tried to keep himself to himself, every month or so the pull of people lured Killy in. A cold beer, a conversation with something besides his truck, and a hot body to sink his cock into…. Like filling the El with gas, sooner or later he'd have to stop and tank up. Then hit the road again.

Even from a distance of five feet, he swore he heard the man's heartbeat, recognized the want in those intelligent eyes, and smelled the heady combination of soap, sweat, cologne, and man. The mix shot an arrow straight to his groin. Tonight's special? Cowboy, with all the trimmings.

For the second time that day, Texas studied Killy's lanky frame. The humor fled his face. "Umm… can I take you to the diner first before we, well, you know?"

The fidgeting, and the bashful gaze connecting before darting away, hit another one of Killy's hot buttons. Shy? How charming. Beneath a layer of faded denim, Killy's cock hardened even more.

With last night's burger a distant memory, Killy nodded. "I reckon I could eat." The El was too loaded down for a passenger, so he crossed the cracked asphalt to a rusted-out Bronco sporting a Texas license plate, following a firm ass. Threadbare jeans left little to the imagination. Tex rounded to the driver's side.

A knot formed in Killy's gut. "Mind if I drive?" He'd come a long way in three years, but still couldn't handle someone else behind the wheel.

"Gonna kidnap me, haul me off somewhere, and have your way with me? No need for all that; I'm willing." Dimples framed a devilish grin.

"Nope, I just prefer to do the driving."

"Then I reckon you'll have to make it up to me, the not-kidnapping thing, 'cause let me tell ya, ever since you walked into the bar I've been fantasizing. And oh hell yeah, you can do the driving. Now and later."

In his ad reply Texas gave his age as twenty-two; right then he looked young and mischievous, totally unlike the timid innocent he'd appeared a moment ago. Killy liked a little spirit in his fucks. Fun times on the horizon.

Mr. Texas Drawl directed him to a diner on the edge of town, a holdover of '50s architecture. No matter where Killy went, like a magnet drawing steel, he always managed to find a clone. They all looked the same, and served the same fare. Sitting inside, he could be in Houston, Jacksonville, or even upstate New York. The sensory ghosts of bacon, coffee, and eggs lingered in the air, the smell from the early morning entrees gradually giving ground to the scent of burgers, fries, and burnt grease.

A booth in the back gave them privacy, and they placed their orders. Killy waited for the inevitable, *"Are you really him?"* Regardless of how he answered, the asker's eagerness eventually succumbed to logic. Killian Desmond died three years ago. All the papers said so.

The bassist didn't disappoint. "You're the real deal, ain't ya?"

Sound bored; don't let him know he hit a nerve. Even so, Killy's heart sped. "Does it make a difference?"

Tex shrugged. "Not really. But if you are, I'm left to wonder why you don't want to be."

Don't want to be summed his life up pretty well. "It's a long story that'd take longer'n I got to tell."

Head cocked to the side, Tex's expression changed from curious to puzzled, eventually settling into accepting. Killy'd love to have been privy to the man's inner dialog. "For the record, I'm glad you're not dead. Are the others still around, or just you?"

Casting wary eyes right and left bought him some time. Should he answer truthfully, or hand out the normal bullshit? The other Triksterz band members had made it quite clear they thought him an imposter. Not even a flicker of doubt showed in this man's eyes. No need to lie. No one would believe this guy anyway. Judging by how comfortably the other three band members talked with each other while ignoring both guitar players, Texas didn't fit in any more than Killian did.

Besides, the burden had been building inside for three long, silent years. Only a handful of people knew the truth, and making money hand over fist ensured their silence. Time to roll the dice and take a gamble. Killy whooshed out a breath. "Just me."

He expected, "I knew it!" and excitement. Instead he got, "Then I'm really sorry about the others. It's hard to lose a brother."

"You've no idea."

The anticipated, *"What really happened?"* didn't come. Rather, "Sorry about your mother, too."

That wound, neither ragged nor fresh, didn't weigh nearly as heavily on Killian's mind. He'd tried, and failed, to stop Mama's downward spiral. At least he'd tried. His brother's death, however... He waved a dismissive hand. "That's the way it goes with addicts. Every fix is practice for that final one." Bad drugs from an unknown source had put an end to *"One day we'll settle down, live like a real family."*

While Killian and Elliot mourned, Mama's manager painted over "Debbie Desmond" on the tour bus with "The Desmond Brothers." Once able to think clearly again, Killy and Elliot presented a united front against the bastard who'd run their lives for far too long. They informed him in no uncertain terms that his client was dead and his services no longer needed. Then they'd hired their own manager and repainted the bus, *Trickster* rising from the ashes of a family's crash and burn.

"Why do you let folks believe you're dead?"

"'Cause I am, as far as they're concerned. I've always been Debbie's boy, or one of the Desmonds. I've been working on it three years now and still haven't the foggiest notion who Killian Desmond is."

"You didn't change your name. Why not? If you're hiding."

"Hiding in plain sight's been working so far. It ain't broke, I ain't fixing it." Besides, Killy's last name alone remained of the world's most dysfunctional family. He'd be damned if he'd give that up.

Tex dropped his line of questioning, changing the topic to something far less uncomfortable. "You still writing songs?"

"Here and there. Not that they'll ever get recorded. Those days are over and done." Give him a few idle minutes and a notepad, and words seemed to find their way from his fingers to the paper. There was no "off" switch to the part of him that lived for making music, the only thing keeping him from trading his half-life for no life.

Their meals arrived and Killy wolfed down his burger and fries in silence, trying to puzzle out the enigma sitting across from him. The guy bore all indications of being a fan, yet didn't stare at him in idolizing fascination. No, he treated Killy like an ordinary man. Killian liked ordinary.

Texas paid their tab, climbed into the Bronco's passenger seat without question, and gave Killian directions. They drove a few miles and turned off the paved road. Row after row of single-wide mobile homes sat baking in the sun, not a tree in sight to offer shade. How the hell did folks even tell 'em apart?

Bile rose in Killian's throat. In his worst nightmares, this would be his life: working nine to five, then coming home to the same run-down home every day. Was that even living?

The tiny trailer they parked in front of had seen better days. Old and battered, it appeared deserted. A faded towel hung from the front window instead of a curtain. "It ain't home, just where I'm sleeping this week," said his host.

Time to stop thinking about the past and get back to the matter at hand: a willing body, and a fine one at that. Tex's nicely rounded ass made a pleasant distraction as he led the way across the yard and up three steps to unlock the door.

Despite its outside appearance, inside the trailer was pleasantly cool. A lone recliner and tiny TV sitting on a plastic milk crate occupied the front room. Nothing else. The place smelled dry and dusty, with the faintest hint of pine cleaner. Okay, he'd seen the sights, now for...

Tex ushered Killy further inside. "Can I get you a beer?"

What is wrong with you, Killian? Fuck the guy, catch a nap, and get on with your life. Socializing is nearly as bad as kissing. You'll never see him again. Just fucking fuck and leave! He knows too much already! "Nah, I'm good."

Tex paused, a "what now?" look in his eyes.

Killy would gladly show him the next step in the dance. He grabbed Tex by the shoulders and slammed him against the nearest wall hard enough to rattle the cabinets in the kitchen a few steps away. The cowboy's masculine scent filled his nose and started a fire in his groin.

Tex grinned. "Oh, you like it rough, huh? I can definitely do rough." That thin layer of dark beard grew close; Killy ducked away.

"What?" Tex asked.

"I don't kiss."

Again a black crow's wing brow questioned him. "Why not?"

"Kissing leads to caring." Just look where caring had gotten Elliot.

"What's so bad about that?"

"If you don't blow your brains out first, you wind up sitting on the front porch, old and gray, wondering how life passed you by."

Tex grasped Killy's jaw, forcing him face to face. A too-perceptive stare bored into Killy, penetrating down to his soul. "Must suck being you."

"It does" remained unspoken.

Tex put his lips within a hair's breadth from Killy's and froze.

Killy could almost taste the beer on the man's breath. His cock ached at the thought. Mouth to mouth, tongue to tongue. He raised his chin. Oh, hell. Tex ducked his head. Damn!

No! Killy didn't want a kiss! And especially not from a man he'd fuck today and forget tomorrow. Time to stop thinking.

Tex's neck made an inviting target, muscles working when he swallowed. Oh yeah. Killy scraped his teeth over the skin above Tex's collar. Sweat and man and slight traces of cologne.

Too many clothes! Killian backed away long enough to yank the T-shirt over Tex's head, then returned to latch his mouth onto one beaded nipple. He worked the bud to full hardness while popping open the button and unzipping Tex's jeans with moves he'd practiced since his teens.

Clothes off!

He reached his hand inside to cup an impressive erection. Oh hell yeah. With one smooth move he pulled Tex's jeans and boxers down, then sank to his knees to take hard flesh into his mouth.

Salty precome hit his tongue. Mouth full of hard cock. He grabbed two handfuls of nicely rounded ass for leverage and took the man all the way in.

Tex stumbled and would have fallen if not for the wall against his back and Killy's grip. "Don't...don't you think we should take this to the bedroom," Tex gasped out.

Not really. Here worked just fine. Or on the floor. Or even in the fucking yard. But if Tex wanted the bed... Killy pulled off. "Lead on."

Tex pulled up his jeans enough to shuffle into the next room.

The bedroom matched the rest of the trailer, with faded wallboard and worn brown carpet. An antique iron bed sat against one wall, covered by a patchwork quilt with cotton leaking from ripped seams, folded back to reveal plain white sheets.

A firm tug on Killy's shirt pulled it from his jeans, and Texas worked a hand, cool against heated flesh, underneath the fabric to caress Killy's bare skin. He slipped the shirt over Killy's head and dropped it on the floor. With the faintest of touches he traced Killy's abs, creeping steadily higher, igniting a fuse to burn straight to Killy's straining erection.

Tex dipped his fingertips beneath Killy's waistband, to gently stroke the head of his cock.

Killy batted Tex's hand away. Oh hell no. In the bedroom, *he* called the shots, the better to keep his casual fucks casual. Tex's will, what he wanted, what he liked, how he treated a man in bed, was too much information. There could be no tender kisses or reverent caresses to dwell on later. Just the slick-slide, skin-slapping-skin of two men whose time together had a fast-approaching expiration date.

Killy toed off his boots and stripped. His clothes lay where they fell. He shoved Tex backward onto the bed to jerk his shoes, jeans and boxers off.

Texas scanned his torso, eyes widening slightly at the sight of the tattoo on his biceps, "Trickster" with a likeness of the band's first album cover. The tat still didn't prove anything. From the first time Killy showed his piece onstage, fans flocked to tattoo parlors across the country and e-mailed him pictures. He'd seen some of them again on a "good art gone bad" website.

But...he didn't have anything to prove. He'd told the truth about who he was. Tex didn't believe, didn't care, or chose to humor the crazy person. Whatever the man's way of thinking, a hard fucking lay in his immediate future.

Tex leaned up and ran a trembling hand over the ropey scar that traveled beneath Killy's Adam's apple, across his chest, and down his belly, stopping shy of his navel. Never saying a word, Texas bent and kissed the ragged reminder of near-death, tracing the jagged line with a hot tongue. One inch higher would have made an honest man of the guy who'd written Killy's obituary.

Tex slipped from the bed and dropped to his knees. A heavy *thump* echoed throughout the trailer. He ran his mouth from Killy's balls to cock tip, taking his time. The Stetson landed on the floor beside him.

Base to tip, base to tip, gentle tongue laps bathed Killy's flesh. Bucking his hips, Killian urged Tex to stop teasing and get down to business. A chuckling laugh vibrated against his belly. Then, opening wide, Tex downed Killy's length in a smooth, wet glide of pure bliss.

With his hands braced on Tex's shoulders, Killy squinted his eyes tightly against the pleasure coursing through him in great, pulsing waves. Tex pulled off with a moist-sounding *pop* and rose gracefully to his feet.

One push against his chest had Tex sprawled on the sheets again. Killy followed him down. Damned if the hot hunk of cowboy stretched beneath him didn't look good. Starting at the neck and working down Tex's torso put Killy's mouth right where he wanted. Finally, after what seemed a small eternity of teasing little licks, Killy opened his mouth and slid all the way down the rigid perfection he'd first seen on the Internet.

Tex bucked, hips thrusting, spurring Killy on. Tightening his lips and humming low in his throat sent vibration through Tex's cock; a drop of salty pre-come rewarded the effort.

Tex moved his fingers from Killy's hair to the mattress, digging in. His body bowed. Oh yes. He was close, real close. Ah, what a perfect cock to lick, but Killy wanted more than just Tex's come in his mouth. He sat back, spectator to Tex's battle with his libido. Tex won by a narrow margin, judging by the dazed, "Wha...?"

He climbed up Tex, who arched up eagerly, his thick cock sliding against Killy's longer, slimmer one. Settling between Tex's legs, their full, heavy sacks connected while Killy ground their erections together.

Their gazes met and held. Moving forward an inch would put the wet press of the man's grin against Killy's. Full lips. Inviting mouth. And inside, the hot slide of tongue to dance with Killy's own. Fuck, he wanted it. Ached for it. Tex turned his head. Killy's mouth landed on a beard roughened cheek. What the fuck? Killy didn't kiss, and twice now he'd wanted to. More than wanted to.

If he dropped his guard, gave in to temptation once, a single kiss might escalate into a primal, insatiable thing that curled his toes and consumed him completely. The last thing he needed was more memories dogging his heels cross-country. He'd had enough of those already. No kissing. No matter that right now Killy would kill or die to plunder Tex's mouth.

Sex. Now that's something Killy understood. He nipped Tex's earlobe as a poor substitute, and thrust against the man beneath him.

Losing his reserved streak in the breathless heat of the moment, Tex ran his hands over the expanse of

Killian's back before grabbing a double handful of ass and pulling them closer together. Hot damn! Forceful! Nice!

Tex scraped his teeth lightly over Killy's neck, worrying the spot just beneath his left ear. Warm breath heated Killy's lobe and a rough hand encased their cocks, frantically working both. "Just let go, take the edge off. We've got all day." Ah, but the man's voice could warm up a Minnesota winter.

Taking the edge off sounded good. And all day sounded even better. But...Wait a damn minute! All day? What happened to "fuck and leave"? Oh, yeah. Tex happened. Time enough to worry about later... well, later. Killian shoved into Tex's hand. All day sounded real good right now.

All day? He focused on the heat in Tex's eyes, the firm grip of the man's hand. *I want to stay all day? Fuck yeah!* Oh, fuck! No time to puzzle out what any of this meant. Lightning struck deep within, faster than a bronc out of the gate. "Ahhhh..." he groaned. Tex stiffened against him, muscles spasming. Precome slicked things up, Tex's hand sliding more easily along their lengths, hurling them both over the edge. Killian rode out wave after wave of shuddering ecstasy. A moan from Tex said he'd come along for the ride.

Finally spent, Killy collapsed beside his bedmate, panting through the aftershocks, heart thudding wildly in his chest.

They lay on their backs on the sweat-soaked sheets, saying nothing, Tex resting a hand on Killy's thigh. That wasn't too bad. Killy reached over to lay his hand on Tex. Touching wasn't as dangerous as kissing, was it? Despite having just come, neither completely lost their erections and they fully revived in no time.

Tex moved his fingers, his slight touches growing demanding, sexual, and he flipped over onto his stomach, jerked a pillow beneath his hips, and offered his ass up like a gift. He reached under the edge of the bed to retrieve a half-full bottle of lube and a battered box of condoms. Maybe he'd been toting them around awhile. Did that mean lots of jacking off and no real sex in this man's recent past? Better make up for lost time.

Killy lubed a finger and worked Tex's hole. Tex pushed back against him with a whimper. It'd been far too long since Killy'd buried himself to the balls in an eager body.

Soon one finger became two, Tex opening up to the invasion, spreading wide in silent invitation. Killy added more lube. Why did he bother? Why go slow? Normally, Tex would be fucked and forgotten by now.

Not going there. Too much thinking. Shut up and fuck. Killy sheathed his flesh in latex and pressed the tip to Tex's entrance. He gripped the man's broad shoulders and slowly eased in. "Damn, you feel good," he breathed out on a slow exhale.

Tex hissed between his teeth.

"Need me to stop?" *Please say no, please say no.*

In answer, Tex lurched back, hard. Killy rammed in to the hilt, in one long, slick move.

"Oh fuck!" He squeezed his eyes tightly shut. Tex's hot channel gripped him like a tight fist.

"Yeah. And put your back into it, why don't ya?"

A man after Killy's own heart. Advance, retreat, advance, retreat. Flesh smacked flesh, the headboard beating a sharp *rap, rap, rap*, against the wall. Sex and Tex's cologne filled Killy's senses, and he angled his strokes, growing closer and not wanting to short-change his partner. Huh? Since when did he care if the guy he plowed enjoyed the plowing or not?

Their rhythm faltered until Tex restored the tempo, slamming his ass against Killy's groin in a frantic one-two beat. "I'm close, so close," he mumbled against the mattress. He wormed a hand under his body. A litany of curses echoed through the room.

Husky groans mingled as Killy drove in all the way, knocking Tex off the pillow. Tex didn't seem to notice, too busy frantically stroking himself.

Killy came with a strangled cry, filling the rubber in hard pulses. Damn! Wave after wave crashed over him. Tex went rigid beneath him, his litany of "Fuck!" and "damn!" muffled by a pillow.

Falling to the side, chest heaving, Killy sucked in air to catch his breath. Damn, that was... Damn. Just damn. Tex rolled over to face him, hardly winded. He studied Killian's face. "Need a beer now?"

The power of speech having fled, Killy managed a nod. Tex peeled the condom off him and disappeared from the room. A flush and running water through thin walls marked his whereabouts.

He returned a few moments later, handing over an uncapped cold one, then sank down on the bed with a beer of his own, with a pillow for a backrest. "We're alone, and you'll be long gone tomorrow. Anything you wanna get off your chest, I'm here."

Killy took in Tex's casual *"don't matter either way to me"* expression, which contradicted the message in those intense brown eyes saying loud and clear, *"You ain't gonna be here at midnight, might as well."*

Why should he tell his story to a stranger? Why the hell not? Without really knowing why, Killy opened his mouth and shared his biggest secret. "You know how the papers said the bus hit a deer on a slick road and crashed off the side of a mountain?"

"Yes. Some say that's bullshit."

"It's bullshit," Killy confirmed.

Tex sipped his beer, staring at the far wall and idly peeling the label. Bits of paper fluff floated down onto the sheet.

Killy grabbed a pillow and mimicked Tex's pose against the headboard. Not facing the man meant he didn't have to look into curious eyes. And if the cowboy asked the next logical question, Killy would shut him down. The minutes ticked away, the only sound the liquid burble of beer down their throats, distant cars, and the hum of an air conditioner deep in the belly of the trailer. The unit banged when it shut off.

Finally, the silence got the better of him. The truth bubbled up inside like molten lava building to erupt. Elliot and the rest of band needed their stories told. "Thank God Mama put off the inevitable overdose until I turned eighteen. Elliot lacked a few weeks of hitting twenty-one. Young and dumb. I think either one of us alone mighta gotten eaten alive, but we had each other, and kinda did okay." More than okay to hear some people tell it, but those folks got their news from the Internet, the glorified story of two young rockers done good. They didn't see the bad side: how anyone who'd ever spoken to Mama for half a second came to squabble over what they could get. "Her record label and manager fought for her estate, such as it was, slapping down an injunction against us performing her songs." Hell, just because she'd taken full credit didn't mean her last six albums weren't a family effort.

"So you wrote more." Tex finished peeling his bottle and let the label flutter to the floor.

Yeah, that much appeared in his and Elliot's public biographies, spin-doctored to say they couldn't bear to perform the old songs without her. "Her band, down to a bunch of fellow druggies by then, weren't worth keeping on. We formed our own." Him and Elliot against the world, thinking the world owed them success after such a crappy beginning.

"Things were going well until we had the misfortune to meet up with Rob Cassen." If he wasn't already dead, Killy would gladly send him straight to Hell.

"Your drummer, formerly with Cleaver."

Killy snorted. "I wish they'd have kept his sorry ass too. To make a long story short, he tried to take over." His gut churned.

"We don't need your brother. We can strike out on our own, just me and you," the asshole had told Elliot.

Thank God Elliot hadn't listened; not that saying no helped him much in the long run. Only, when Killy found out the guy's plans and tried to toss Rob out of the band, Elliot and his too-big heart talked Killy into giving the fucker another chance. Biggest damn mistake of Killy's life.

"I wasn't having none of it. I'd have fired his ass after a month, but Elliot insisted he stay on. Turns out the bastard sweet-talked his way into my brother's bed. Elliot was too much like Mama, trusting the wrong people and getting used for his trouble."

What had Elliot's unknown father been like? A scholarly type who caved regularly to bullies, giving poor Elliot a double-dose of gullible? Mama simply called him "right place, right time." Both a blessing and a curse, Killian's father, "an alcoholic one night stand who managed to last nearly a year," took bull-headed son-of-a-bitch to new heights, a trait most said bred as true as Killy's sky-blue eyes. But at least Papa Amos pretended to be a father, even letting Elliot tag along on visitations, though he never quite grasped basic parenting concepts like six-years-olds shouldn't have coffee with breakfast.

"I started seeing things—bruises, cuts." Killian cast an anxious glance to Tex, watching for a reaction.

Tex kept his poker face firmly in place and gave nothing away.

What the fuck had gotten into him? Killy couldn't seem to shut up. "Me and Elliot, we'd been through a lot, and always, always stayed best buds. All of a sudden he stopped talking to me, started coming late to practice, and something had to give."

"No, I don't want to talk about it. Nothing's wrong! Would you get off my damned back?" Elliot wrapping his arms around himself didn't quite hide the bruises, and a cowboy hat pulled low didn't disguise the anguish in his eyes.

Fuck, if only Killy hadn't given up and stalked off. If only he'd insisted a little more the first time he'd seen the abuse.

Tex sipped his beer, quietly listening while stroking the back of Killian's free hand with his thumb.

Killy watched the thumb stroking over his skin, so calming for so small a gesture. "It took some doing, but I convinced him to get rid of Rob. They broke up after nearly five years, but we kept the asshole on 'til we could hire another drummer. Our last night in Asheville, North Carolina piled on the straw that broke the camel's back."

"What happened?"

It took a moment for the words to come. "By then Elliot was a beaten man. He didn't smile like he used to. He played music, but no longer from the heart. And he quit talking about the future." Killy shook his head. "Elliot, with so many dreams and plans. He'd stopped living long before he died." And Killy hadn't saved him either time.

Now Killy sat in a rundown mobile home with a guy he barely knew, spilling his guts—the closest he'd come to confession in years. "Rob showed up too strung-out to play, ranting and raving about Elliot leaving him for Ace, our keyboard player. Pure, unadulterated bullshit." Poor Ace. He'd been a good friend, and sure the hell didn't deserve to die so young. "We wound up canceling the concert. I laid into the bastard, told him to get his no-account ass out of my sight, and threatened to kill him if he ever spoke to my brother again—and I meant it. He stomped off without a word."

Several moments passed before Tex broke the silence. "Since they found his body on the bus, I reckon he crossed your path again."

Killy swallowed hard and nodded. This part he'd never told another soul, letting everyone believe there'd been an accident and that he didn't remember a damned thing. Weren't enough drugs in the world to make him forget, Lord knew he'd tried. "We were cruising along through the mountains when the driver spotted a man standing in the road trying to flag us down. Ace and Elliot were neck deep in a poker game in the back of the bus, and I sat up front, talking to the driver. He slammed on the brakes and opened the door, and lo and behold, Rob hopped on, looking all pitiful, asking if we'd give him a lift to Chattanooga. The others felt sorry for the motherfucker and let him on."

If only they'd just kept going, leaving Rob standing in the rain, or better yet, run over his sorry ass.

"I kept an eye out, but he didn't so much as look at Elliot. I musta dozed off, 'cause I woke up to the bus driver slamming on the brakes and Rob screaming." Killy closed his eyes, opening them again to avoid the images forming behind his lids, burned there for all eternity. "Rob had Elliot by the throat, slamming his head against the wall. Ace was slumped over in his seat, blood pouring from his nose."

Tears leaked from Killy's eyes. He wiped them away with a swipe of his hand. Always before he'd hidden them; this time they fell freely. "I tried to pull him off, I really tried..." He trailed off into sobs. *Elliot. Sweet, soft-hearted Elliot.*

Once more Tex leaned over the side of the bed, trading a now-empty beer bottle for a handful of tissues. His comforting arm around Killy's neck pulled him close, holding on through the worst. Man, it felt good to be held. With Mama and Elliot gone, and Killy's father who-knew-where, he'd faced tragedy alone, with no arms to hold him, no one to tell him things would work out. No one to...

"Thanks." Killy let Tex wipe his face.

"You don't have to tell me if you don't want to."

No one had ever spoken so kindly before. "I want to. I don't have a clue why, but I want to." Resting his head on the offered shoulder, Killian nuzzled into the embrace, drenching Tex's bare skin with three years' worth of pent-up agony.

"The driver stopped the bus and ran to help. Rob jumped up and stormed past us. Elliot was so still. I couldn't see him breathing." Killy choked on the words, squeezing them out around the heart lodged in his throat. "I... I tried to help him...."

Elliot! Elliot! Don't leave me, brother!

Tex clasped his shoulder, a solid tie to the here

and now. Killian grasped that hand, hanging on for all he was worth. He took a deep breath. Time to exorcise his personal demons once and for all by sharing them with another. "I left it to the driver to stop that asshole. Next thing I know, we're barreling down the highway, and... nothing. For a split second I didn't hear a thing, no tires on pavement, no humming engine, nothing. Then we fell."

Screaming, searing hot pain. "Elliot! Elliot!" Screeching metal, an explosion... silence.

"I woke up in intensive care two days later. The papers already reported the whole band dead, and I decided...."

"If it weren't broke you weren't gonna fix it," Tex finished for him. Killian nodded against Tex's shoulder.

"Rob, Ace, the driver, all gone. According to the coroner, Elliot died of traumatic asphyxiation. I fell asleep for a few minutes, and that's all it took. The wreck didn't kill him, Rob did with his bare fucking hands. Then finished the job with the rest of the band by driving us of a cliff. Son-of-a-bitch had enough meth in his system to keep us all partying for a week."

"And you blame yourself for the whole damned thing."

"Most of it, anyway."

"If I told you it wasn't your fault would you believe me?"

"Probably not." Killy dabbed at his nose with a tissue. Damn but Tex's arm felt good around his shoulder.

"Then it's up to you to convince yourself, but Killy?"

"Yeah?"

"You stood by your brother. You did what you could for him. Never forget that."

"I shoulda..."

"Shh..." Tex placed a finger over Killy's lips. "You did all you could do. You're just a man after all. You loved your brother and took care of him the best you could."

"I tried. I really tried."

"Is that why you keep moving? So you'll never get attached, never settle down, 'cause then you'll run the risk of losing someone else?"

How did the man get to be so damned smart? "I got tired of the legal mumbo-jumbo, folks wanting me to sign this and sign that, my manager wanting me to form another band, Rob and Ace's families filing lawsuits, tying up assets. Everybody and their brother hoped to make a profit off of three good men losing their lives." Killy scrubbed his hands over his face, day-old stubble rasping against his palms. "Makes me sick to my stomach. When I'd had enough, I hired the best lawyer I could find and got the hell out. Now I keep my head down, don't live like a rock star, and avoid ATMs and such that might give away where I am. My name doesn't trigger any red flags with those who know I'm alive, 'cause they'd never expect me to show up on stage in some rundown bar, playing backup for little more than drinks and tips. Last I heard, there were at least four of us billing ourselves as Killian Desmond."

"I knew it was the real you," Tex replied. "Hell, sight unseen, I'da known it the second you started playing. Nobody rocks like you do. You play from the heart. And not many lead guitarists that I know of play electro-acoustic. It gives your music a distinct sound."

Killian took a deep breath and barked out a bitter laugh. "For all the good it does me."

A smile peeked through Tex's scruff. "I've sung backup for you in the car more times than I can count. Funny, you're alone, but you and your music kept me from being lonely during the worst times in my life."

He didn't say another word, simply held Killian through another bout of sobbing that slowly gentled into weak, sniffling hiccups. Killy fell asleep to a softly sung melody.

Killy switched off the Bronco.

"You sure you're up to this?" Tex asked from the passenger seat.

A few more cars filled the parking lot—not a crowd, but more than just the band. The night air thudded with a hard bass beat, and neon lights lit the bar's windows. Another night, another show, then move on. Somehow, after an afternoon with Tex and waking up to a smile and a mound of scrambled eggs and bacon, moving on didn't sound as good as it had earlier. But to get there, he first had to play his band's old songs.

Killy huffed out a sigh. "No, I'm not. But what can I do?"

"We could leave now, beat traffic by driving at night."

We. Not *you.* For a moment Killian almost said yes. But Tex didn't mean it; he'd only been trying to make Killy feel better. But why? People didn't do things for him, they expected him to do for them. And if he hightailed it now, Tex would be the one shining star in a mediocre band. Killy didn't owe the band shit...but he owed Tex for being there, no matter how short a time.

"It can't be that bad, can it? A few hours, a few songs." Killy tried for a smile and failed. Too out of practice. "Reckon we should duct tape the singer's mouth? Might improve the show."

A fist pounded on the window. Killy jumped. The keyboard player shouted through the glass. "I'm glad to see you! Kevin's puking his guts out and can't sing. We might have to cancel."

"Kevin?" Oh, the poor excuse for a lead singer. Killy shot a glance toward Tex to find the man staring back at him. "Well, there goes the evening."

The man outside hollered, "I heard you sing, man. You sound like Killian Desmond. Would you still play? Some of us need the money."

Killy rolled the window down. "If I sing, who's got backup?" All Trickster's songs were written for two parts, his and Elliot's. They wouldn't work as solos.

"I got your back," Tex said. "I've backed you up before, remember? The bar's a bit bigger than my Bronco, but I reckon I'll make do." He grinned. Damn but Killy could get used to the man flashing those teeth.

Still, singing along with a CD in the car couldn't compare with singing live. Killy gazed out at the sparse cars. Not like they'd have much of an audience, and if Tex sang like he did everything else, they might have a decent night. This time Killy managed a bit more of a smile. "You're on."

Why the fucking hell had he agreed to this? Killian glared at a few cowboy-types playing pool, or more interested in picking up women than in a live show. The band finished their tuning and someone silenced the blaring jukebox.

Tex stepped close. His breath gusted over Killian's cheek. "I think it's time to wake 'em up, don't you?"

Killy picked a few notes. No one turned toward the stage, and no one shut up. Hell, he couldn't hear himself think in here, and if he'd brought a pistol, he'd shoot that damned disco ball off the motherfucking ceiling. He picked a few more notes. Still nothing.

I'll fix their asses.

Nothing sent crowds from near-comatose to on their feet better than "Highway". But fuck, Killy could use a beer or two, or six or seven, before playing a song so bound and determined to crush the remaining shards of his heart.

Music raged inside of him, a tsunami pulling back from shore. When the tide turned, he'd be swept away. Given the choice between flailing in the water and riding the waves, he'd ride. He took a deep breath, willing the familiar stage rush to get him through the next few hours. *One, two, three, four... breathe in, breathe out.*

They didn't deserve the best he had to offer, but the song wanted out.

32

Scree, scree, scree, screeeee! He hit the opening riff and stopped. In the suddenly quiet room a pool ball clicked against another. Every eye focused on Killy, like a thousand times before. He'd lived for the attention, the adoration, the music. Now he couldn't care less if thousands heard him or one. His soul had started spewing back at the trailer, and if he didn't get the rest of the poison out he just might lose his mind.

"I think you've made a point," Tex murmured.

Not a damned one of these sons of bitches deserved the sacrifice he made, gifting them with a song he'd once vowed to never play again. In his mind Ace filled the void, a run on the keyboard echoing off the walls.

Let's do this, Elliot whispered from his memories.

He turned and nodded to his band...not his band... whatthefuckever.

This one's for you, boys. Now to show the people of wherever the hell he was how real men rocked. He fired the riff again, quicksilver fingers dancing on his guitar strings. Tex joined in. The keyboard player missed his cue but made a quick recovery, and the drummer came in on time. Good. He might not have to hurt them.

Killian opened his mouth and out came the familiar words, sung by rote. What the fuck?

No, no, no, no, no! This wasn't the song he'd written, this was the poor excuse for a ballad cover bands destroyed in hopes of one day getting it right. Once more he stopped. *Get the mood right, motherfucker, or get off the stage.* He might as well be lip-synching if he couldn't get more emotion into the words.

He stared out over a spellbound audience who didn't have sense enough to know how badly he'd screwed up. Idiots. They stood in the palm of his hand, his to toy with as he did his guitar.

Tonight he'd take them to Heaven or send them to Hell. *Spin the wheel folks, which will it be?*

He owed it to himself, Trickster, and hell, even his guitar, to do right by the memory of days gone by.

He alone survived to carry on the legacy. And carry on he would.

Once more he nodded to his now-silent band. Tex raised an eyebrow in question, but kept his comments to himself. Good man. No time for talking now.

Killy fired the riff directly at his audience. They screamed and clapped. He played through the first verse, the lump in his throat holding back his words. Beside him Tex improvised, throwing in chords Killy hadn't written, right where they needed to be.

On the second time around he threw back his head.

He didn't sing. No, he cut his heart open and bled his soul onto the stage. Every word slashed like a razor. The club, the people who'd nothing better to do than stand around and listen, even the tacky disco ball, disappeared.

"Highway" wasn't a ballad of remorse and regret, but an anthem of triumph, a man's exultation in living by his own rules. The tempo slowed, the chorus approached.

"...*And on the highway I was born, it's there I'll meet my end.*"

The purest, sweetest tenor wrapped around Killy's voice, caressing, teasing, scraping away the rough edges until two voices became one. He kept his eyes to the front, for fear he'd turn around and see his past staring over his shoulder. He finished the chorus with chills on his arms.

Tex's voice quieted while Killy wailed his heart out on the next verse. In his mind the highway stretched boundless before him, more vast than the ocean. Hop on a bus, keep going, find out what's over the next hill, and the next, and the next.

A shoulder bumped his, then, back to back, he and Tex sank into the chorus. Tex's notes reverberated through Killy's shoulders, letting him feel as well as hear. This wasn't Elliot, who Killy had to protect, and whose delicate tones got overrun if Killy wasn't careful.

Tonight the brakes were off. Killy let loose, filling the room with his voice, pouring out his bottle of pain.

Tex matched him note for note, and on the final verse, instead of letting Killy solo, Tex harmonized like they'd practiced for years. Eyes closed, Tex's heat against his back, together they breathed new life into old words.

The music took him, and the rest of the band had to follow if they could, and Tex could, he kept up through every twist and turn.

Every now and then Killy opened his eyes, each time more people stood before him. He shut them all out again. Tonight wasn't about them. Tonight wasn't for them. Tonight was...tonight was Killy's. He sang for himself and the lost dreams and for Elliot. For Ace and for an unsung bus driver whose name didn't make the papers.

The audience served as Killian's punching bag, he'd punch them in the heart and the nads and maybe give them enough sugar to make it hurt twice as much when he punched them again.

The last notes died. Killy dropped to the floor on his knees, every ounce of strength poured into the song.

It took a moment for the thunderous applause to penetrate his overwhelmed brain, complete with stomping and caterwauls. What? Do what? A sea of faces swam before his vision, cheering, screaming.

Tex had his back and now was offering a hand. And "possibly more" rang through his memory from the hookup ad... "You okay?"

Killy nodded. "I...I think so."

Adrenaline coursed through his veins. If he didn't start playing, he'd punch someone for real. He started in on the next song: "Like You Mean It". To spice up the act he reinserted the words deleted from the censored album: "*Fuck me* like you mean it." And fuck anyone who didn't like it!

Piercing whistles met his words. Hey, there weren't nearly this many people when he'd started playing. He didn't slow down. At a smile and a wink from Tex, he transitioned into the next song, "You're

Not the Devil, You're Worse", to lighten the moment with a little hard-driven humor.

Elliot's favorite song. Tex stepped into Elliot's role, easily scaling a vocal range few men could manage. Elliot. Killy's brother. His best friend. A tear trailed down his cheek to mingle with the sweat pouring from his brow. He wiped it away with the back of his hand.

Music thrummed through him, awakening something within he'd thought long dead. *I'm alive. I'm alive!* It took him several chords to realize the song had ended and he played on alone.

"Buy you a beer?" Tex asked.

They took a break and a man walked over with beers for the band. Ignoring the others, he addressed Killy and Tex. "We haven't met, but I'm Merle, I own this place. And you boys are welcome here anytime you like. Anytime. I ain't had a crowd like this for years."

Killy sucked down half his beer. Staying wasn't in the cards.

"If you don't mind, would you play 'Highway' again for me? It's always been a personal favorite of mine. Broke my heart when Trickster crashed the bus." Someone called and the man ambled off in a hurry.

Killy and Tex finished their beers. The other two band members kept their distance, holding court with admirers a few feet away. Neither one would go home alone tonight. Men and women buzzed around Killy and Tex like gnats, none bold enough to come closer. Something wild and electric surrounded them, an aura of raw energy, terrifying and mesmerizing all at once. Fucking amazing.

Screaming met Killy's ears the moment he—not so much took the stage, but pounced for the kill. He teased out a few notes of the opening riff, only to start again and add a few more. *Oh, yeah, I'll give you what you want, but on my terms.*

"Anything in particular you wanna hear?" he asked the audience, knowing damned good and well what they'd say.

"Highway!" they screamed.

He cupped a hand to his ear. "What's that? I can't hear you?"

"Highway!" they screamed louder.

He turned toward the bass guitarist. "I can't make out what they're saying. Can you?"

Tex laughed and answered with his fingers on his guitar strings. The drummer tapped out a beat behind them.

Killian stood on the edge of the stage, feeling the heat and adoration from the crowd at his feet, and soaked up their love like electricity, recharging all the energy he'd expended in the earlier set. In the old days he'd be picking out the night's entertainment at this point. A woman lifted her T-shirt to bare her breasts while a tight cluster of women around her reached for him. *No, thank you. I've got it covered.*

"Highway! Highway!" An entire roomful of people took up the chant.

He glanced over at Tex. "They're starting to sound a little restless."

Tex grinned and chatted back, playing off Killy like Elliot used to. "Well, I reckon we better give 'em 'Highway'."

Killy unleashed his soul, wrapped up in music.

The rest of the band picked the night's partners and left. Tex and Killy grabbed two barstools and jammed. Folks came up and took their picture or dropped tips on the stage, but Killy didn't care. Nothing existed outside the music and the man at his side. No matter how complicated the chord, give Tex a second, and he'd add counterpoint.

"Last call!" the bartender shouted for the third time.

Fuck. Time to go. Killy pocketed more cash from the owner than he'd expected, not to mention tips. "Since you're lead singer," Merle told him, adding a wink. A night's wages, and possibly more to entice Killy back. The man should've saved his money.

Without thinking, Killy followed Tex to the Bronco. Oh. Here's where they'd part company. Time to return to his sad little life, in a world where he used to be Killian Desmond.

"Come back to the trailer with me?" Tex's eyes glittered in the dark parking lot, with only a few street lamps to drive back the gloom. A scattering of cars remained beside the Bronco and the El.

What good would it do to postpone the inevitable?

"Look, we've been playing for hours, and you're rushing on adrenaline," Tex said, in that no-nonsense way of his. "When you crash, it's gonna hurt. You need some sleep." Killy didn't resist the hand on his shoulder when Tex helped him into the Bronco.

He lay back in the seat. Hell, letting the man drive once wouldn't hurt. Tex climbed behind the steering wheel and fired up the engine. "Where'd you learn to sing and play like that?" Killy asked.

A quiet mumble barely reached his ears. "I had me a band once." At the next red light Tex exhaled hard and leaned over to dig a CD case out of the glove compartment. He flipped on the overhead light and passed the case to Killy. "My stepfather was a preacher who found a way to make his wife and four stepsons earn their keep."

Killy stared at the CD case. Raptured Roses? What kind of name was that? Oh, gospel band. No wonder he hadn't heard of them. Five smiling faces graced the front cover, an older couple and three young men, one probably around thirteen, the other two likely in their late teens or early twenties. Three, not four, and none were Tex.

Killy flipped the case over to read the back. "Reverend T.S. Rose, with his wife Anna and three sons..."

This time, there was no mistaking Tex's snort. "I buy their CDs 'cause it's the only way I still get to see my brothers."

What the fuck? "It's hard to lose a brother" Tex had said. And he knew firsthand. Maybe not the way Killy did, but the results were the same.

Not that Tex would be the first gay man tossed out by family. Must've been hell hiding that part of himself from the preacher. No way would Killy's family, as fucked up as they were, have ever turned their backs. No fucking way. Tex had not one, but three brothers, and a mom, still alive, but just as gone to him as Elliot was to Killy.

"How long you been on your own?"

"Since I was nineteen." Tex didn't offer more; a growl in his voice said now wasn't the time to push.

Nineteen huh? That would have been about the time "Highway" went gold. *You and your music have kept me from being lonely during the worst times in my life.* Had the man clung to Trickster to get him through being cast out?

If Killy guessed right, they'd been alone about the same length of time. Too damned long.

They didn't speak the rest of the way to the trailer. What could he say?

They hadn't drunk much at the bar, and burned off any alcohol playing. Still, Killy barely kept his eyes open by the time Tex shut the engine off and led him inside. He peeled his clothes off and collapsed on the bed. The moment Tex's mouth found his, all weariness fled.

Killy jerked, old habits kicking online at the brush of lips. Tex withdrew. Callused hands stroked his arms, and Tex's hairy chest tickled Killy's nearly hairless pecs.

Something slow and sensual played on the portable CD player by the bed. Tex kept time with the music, running his lips around Killy's jaw to get to his ear, but avoided his mouth. He caught Killy's earlobe between his teeth, nipping hard enough to cause a gasp. With teeth and tongue he worked Killy's throat and Adam's apple, worshipping the expanses of skin, taking his time.

An unrestrained madman on bass, a thoughtful lover in bed, a hell of a cook, and a caring man to boot. What was the guy's angle? What was he after?

No need to fret. Come morning, the detour ended with Killy's return to the road.

A hand on his ass brought Killy out of his musings. He spread his thighs without thought. How long since he'd bottomed? Nothing registered now but Tex warming him up. He grabbed the man by the wrist. "No."

Without questioning Tex put the condom he'd held to his own cock on Killy's. "It's not that," Killy said. Why explain? What did it matter? "I got broncs to ride in two days, and I haven't done this in a while."

Tex pulled his lips back in a smile. "Rain check?"

"Sure." Wait. Killy couldn't promise a rain check. In a few hours he wouldn't be here.

Oh, but the twin swells of cowboy ass called to him, and a ride so much sweeter than a bronc. He buried his face in the furry mat on Tex's chest, inhaling sweat, cologne, tobacco smoke, and stale beer. Smelled like home. He pushed his cowboy back on the mattress and knelt between his knees. A little warm up, a little slicking up, and drive home. Home. Where was that?

For now home existed in a man's hairy arms, sinewy muscles holding him close. In pants and grunts, and muffled curses. In the step, shuffle, turn of the mating dance. Killy sang the melody with his body, playing Tex with every stroke, every grunt, every out, out, out, too far, now back in.

Tex rocked against him, adding harmony with his hands drawing Killy close, and his legs hooked around Killy's thighs. A chorus of squeaky bed springs joined in, and "Oh!" and "ah!" and "oh my God!"

They'd met less than a day ago, yet in perfect accord they came together in a carnal two-step, dancing like old lovers, long experienced in the perfect place to caress or bite.

Killy fought to hold on, to prolong the moment. Tex felt too good, loved too hard. Like on the stage, he didn't just play, everything he did he gave his all.

Lucky Killy. With a cry he came hard.

Tenor joined his bass, echoing off the walls.

Killy awoke to the soft strumming of a guitar. A voice as rich as chocolate crooned about lovers done wrong. Singing? Guitar? Oh shit! Morning. Killy had stayed all night.

He followed the tune into the kitchen.

"Good morning. Sorry, did I wake ya?" Tex sat on the edge of a kitchen chair, in just his jeans, a beat-up acoustic in his hands. He never missed a lick and moved on to the next chord.

"What's that you're playing?"

"A little something I'm working on." He went back to picking.

Killy pulled the other chair out from under the two-seater table and plopped down. "Mind if I hear?"

Tex dipped his head, the shyness from yesterday reappearing. "I don't rightly know if I ought to. I mean, you being you and all."

"I'm just a man. Isn't that what you told me yesterday?" The melody lodged in Killy's head, and already chords formed in his mind, a keyboard and drums joining in.

Fingers strumming softly on the strings, Tex closed his eyes and began to sing. Images formed in Killy's brain, staring outside, waiting for the rain to stop to get on the road again, eager to escape a love gone belly up. He tapped out a beat with his fingers on the tabletop. Oh, man! If he put in a run here, and there he'd add... "I need my guitar. I'd go get it myself, but..." He waved a hand toward his naked body. Normally, he tried to hide his vivid scars. Tex looked right through them.

41

"That'd make the neighbors talk. Hold this." Tex handed Killy his guitar and traipsed out the front door, only to return a few moments later with Killy's guitar case.

Killy didn't ever bother to tune up. When Tex started playing again, he joined in. And on a whim, he added harmony to Tex's melody. As in the bar, their voices merged like they'd sung together for years. He didn't want the song to stop, for then the spell might break and he'd return to his aimless wondering, a shell of who he used to be.

For a little while two lonely men didn't have to be alone—until the music ran out. They played the whole thing through three times before Tex gave him a rueful smile. "We're both borrowing time, aren't we?"

Nice to know Killy wasn't alone in his thinking. With a sigh, he put his guitar away. He gazed into his host's eyes. What could he say? *It's been nice? See ya 'round?*

Tex placed his guitar aside, watching Killian the whole time. "You catch a shower and get dressed."

What the fuck? Was Texas tossing him out? "What time is it now?"

"Eleven thirty."

Fuck. He'd planned to be on the road by four. Hell, they probably hadn't gotten in until three. Killy showered. He turned off the water to the sound of a house being torn apart. What the hell was the man doing out there? He pulled yesterday's clothes back on and stepped into the hallway. Tex emerged from the bedroom, bearing two loaded pillowcases. Killy followed him into the living room.

The Stetson-crowned cowboy strode purposefully out to the Bronco, returning a second and third time, carrying out boxes and a stuffed duffle bag. He dragged a cooler from under the kitchen table and dumped the refrigerator's contents inside—mostly beer.

"Twelve o'clock; we need to get moving." Tex surveyed the room and picked a handful of change off the television. Looked like Killy wasn't the only one moving on. Where was the guy headed? And why did Killy want to know?

They drove to the Stallion in silence. Several times he opened his mouth, but nothing came to mind to say. If he wanted to be back on the road so bad, why did his heart hurt?

This was it, the end of the line. The rodeo beckoned, and endless days of same ole, same ole. For a little while, for a moment in time, he'd gotten to pretend life could go on. He'd sung again. From the heart. And lightning hadn't struck him for playing without his old band.

Tex parked out from of the Rarin' Stallion. "My vehicle's bigger than yours, has four-wheel drive, and is roomy enough to sleep in. Get what you want out of your El Camino." A few cars littered the parking lot. Probably, like Killy, the owners had found another ride the night before.

Wait. What? "What do you mean?"

"Exactly what I said." Tex locked eyes with Killy. "Get your stuff and let's go. I'm coming with you—if you'll let me." His gaze never wavered.

"You don't want this." Killy had to be the voice of reason, even though in his heart he was tired of traveling alone. "I never stay anywhere long. I'm always on the move."

Tex reached into his pocket and extracted a crumpled pack of gum. He popped a strip into his mouth and gave a few good chews. "What does this taste like?"

Kill scratched his head. "How the hell am I supposed to know?"

"Exactly."

"Huh?"

"If you ain't the one doing the chewing, how can you know what it tastes like?" Tex paused. "If you ain't the one doing the living, how can you know what I want? Ain't one damned thing keeping me here. I was passing through myself when the Bronco broke down. I stayed long enough to get it fixed, and planned to leave in a few days anyhow. I'd hoped in answering your ad I might find myself a passenger for the trip. Gets mighty lonely riding alone." He grinned. "Besides, I like the way you fuck. I also think you could use some company, too."

"Why?"

"Why what?"

"Why say you'll come with me? You don't even know where I'm going."

"All the places I've been, I know what they're like." Texas shrugged, like he shouldn't have to explain. "But anywhere I go with you will be new."

Damn but Killian loved this man's twisted logic.

Never questioning the newly voiced authority, Killy dug his few belongings out of the El Camino, wrestling his saddle into the Bronco's back seat. He did a double-take at the saddle already nestled between a box and a sleeping bag. As an afterthought, he returned to the El and ejected the Trickster CD he'd been listening to on the way down.

"Where are we going?" Tex asked as he slammed the Bronco's rear door.

Killy only hesitated a minute before climbing behind the steering wheel. "Denver rodeo. Between Mama and Papa, I could play guitar and ride a horse before I lost my first tooth. I'm signed up for a bronc riding event."

"As Killian Desmond?"

"Nah, I use Papa's last name. On the circuit, I'm Killy Amos. We might even meet up with the old fart. He still shows up and hangs out with me every now and then." Killy glanced at the Rarin' Stallion. Tonight folks would show up hoping to see him and Tex again. They could stay here, earn enough to get by. The owner liked them. Or they could find out where the road led.

"What about the gig?" he asked.

"The asshole's bound to get better and want his job back. Do you really wanna play second banana to someone else butchering your songs? Besides, I reckon I got enough money to tide us over until you win big or we find somewhere else to play, if money's troubling you."

"Good point." Killy started the Bronco and turned to face Tex. "You sure about this?"

"I'm sitting in my truck with a man I just met and everything I own piled in back. Don't I look sure?"

Killian studied his new lover's profile while Tex stared straight ahead through the windshield. "Don't you wanna look back on what you're leaving?"

"What's behind me ain't important, unless you wanna sell your truck before we go."

"Three hundred dollar piece of shit or the open road? Let's go."

A bright grin lit up Tex's face. "By the way, Killian, my real daddy rode the rodeo too. Reckon it's too late for me to sign up for bronc riding?" He patted his well-used ass. "Um... in a day or so?"

Two days ago bronc riding looked good, hanging out with the old crowd until the season ended in the fall. But last night relit the fire in Killian's blood. He belonged on a stage, singing his heart out for the masses. One phone call would set the ball in motion. He and his newfound bassist could hit Denver and keep on going, be in LA before long. "I've been thinking."

"Yeah?"

What are you doing, Killy? You just met this guy! "We sound good together."

"I thought so. Those folks last night did too."

You're out of your fucking mind, man! Stop! Killy shushed his inner doubter. "Have you ever thought about joining another band? A real one, not guys like these." Killy flapped his hand at the club.

"It'd be nice to one day show my family I got by fine without them."

Killy's heart sped. "You and me? You'd do it?" He'd contact his manager, arrange auditions for a keyboardist and drummer. Start practicing the compositions languishing on his laptop. But first, to secure his bass player.

"You mean play like we did last night? All the time? Damn, but that was like an orgasm on stage."

Killy listened, but the inner voice that normally sent him running to the hills at the first sign of permanence remained silent. "There's a reporter hangs out at the rodeo. Nice guy, never made the big time. I was thinking..."

"Bout giving him the scoop of a lifetime? Killian Desmond done returned from the dead."

"Something like that."

Tex grabbed his hand and squeezed.

The first honest smile in three years stretched across Killy's mouth. "Mike?" So he'd remembered the name after all. Mike. Mike Rose. And Killian Desmond. They had all the way to Denver to decide on a band name, and to plan Killy's resurrection. His manager would think Christmas came early.

Now, one more thing to do to make his new start complete. He cleared his throat and tried again. "Mike, I reckon I'll take that kiss now."

"You sure?"

Killian answered the only way he knew how. He grabbed the collar of Mike's T-shirt and dragged him halfway into the driver's seat to seal their lips together.

Mike let out a surprised grunt and Killy took advantage, plunging his tongue into the man's mouth. He tasted of peppermint, the open road, and of no longer being alone.

And like Killy had feared, the one touch of lips led to a dance of tongues, weakening and strengthening his resolve all in one, while the stereo played.

"And on the highway I was born, it's there I'll meet my end..."

৯৯ ৯৯ ৯৯

About the Author

You will know Eden Winters by her distinctive white plumage and exuberant cry of "Hey, y'all!" in a Southern US drawl so thick it renders even the simplest of words unrecognizable. Watch out, she hugs!

Driven by insatiable curiosity, she possibly holds the world's record for curriculum changes to the point that she's never quite earned a degree but is a force to be reckoned with at Trivial Pursuit.

She's trudged down hallways with police detectives, learned to disarm knife-wielding bad guys, and witnessed the correct way to blow doors off buildings. Her e-mail contains various snippets of forensic wisdom, such as "What would a dead body left in a Mexican drug tunnel look like after six months?" In the process of her adventures she has written fourteen m/m romance novels, has won several Rainbow Awards, was a Lambda Awards Finalist, and lives in terror of authorities showing up at her door to question her Internet searches. When not putting characters in dangerous situations she's a mild-mannered business executive, mother, grandmother, vegetarian, and PFLAG activist.

Find Eden's other works at www.edenwinters.com or contact her at edenwinters@gmail.com.

Other titles from Rocky Ridge Books

From Eden Winters:

Summer Boys
Tinsel and Frost
The Telling
Night Watch

The Match Novellas
The Match Before Christmas
Fanning the Flames
A Lie I Can Live With

The Diversion Novels
Diversion
Collusion
Corruption
Manipulation
Redemption
Reunion
Suspicion

From P.D. Singer

The On Call Shorts
On Call: Afternoon
On Call: Dancing
On Call: Crossroads
Training Cats

Spokes (novel)
Donal agus Jimmy (novella)
Otter Chaos
Concierge Service

A MATTER OF WHEN

Wealth. Fame. Gold record. Hookers and Cocaine front man Henri Lafontaine has it all... including a control freak manager, band members who smile as they sharpen blades for his back, and last but damn well not least, a fan out to steal his heart. Literally. Trying to write hit songs and plan a comeback in the midst of the hi-fi white noise of LA feels more like watching his world implode, until he's offered a month in the Colorado Rockies for vocal coaching.

Sebastian Unger's rich, classically trained tenor inpsires wicked thoughts. More than a pretty choir boy, he cracks the whip without hesitation to drive tattooed bad boy Henri to give his all to his music. Working, fighting, and finally establishing a fragile peace, they find inspiration and perhaps more in each other. But the clock is ticking. Time will pull Henri back to the grit and gold of LA's mean streets and fame machine, while Sebastian must return to the opera circuit, where a mysterious man known as "the patron" holds far too much sway. Only the trust they've built on a handful of notes bridges their two worlds... and shields them from malice.

DIVERSION

Ex-con turned drug enforcement agent Lucky Lucklighter has a rooky to train and a pill-mill to bust, but noob Bo Schollenberger has a thing or two to teach Lucky.

COLLUSION

Bo and Lucky go undercover in a children's cancer hospital where some heartless bastard's profiteering from tragedy. Heartbreak and disaster may catch them first.

CORRUPTION

Breaking the pipeline on a psychosis-inducing designer drug puts Bo into motorcycle leathers and a new persona. Lucky'd better save his worries about who Bo's becoming for after they survive.

MANIPULATION

Lucky's old life called, and it wants him back. With Bo as hostage, Lucky has little choice but to answer.

SPOKES BY P.D. SINGER

Pro cyclist Luca Biondi lives for the race. For the star of Team Antano-Clark, victory lies within his grasp—if he can outdistance 200 other hopefuls, avoid suspicion from race officials, and keep his lieutenant more friend than foe. Luca also has secrets, and eyes for amateur cyclist and journalist Christopher Nye.

Christopher understands Luca's need to keep their relationship under wraps, but chafes at hiding in the shadows of his lover's career. He's ready to cheer Luca's victories, but he knows too well how triumph can turn to tears. While Christopher's heart sees Luca the man, his inner journalist—and his editor—sees the cycling world's biggest scoop.

From the jagged curves of the Colorado Rockies to the viciously steep Belgian hills, Luca can ride out any bumps—except rumors.

A few words in the wrong ear could crash everything. With miles between them, hints of scandal, and Luca's fierce need to guard his reputation, a journalist might have to let go of the biggest story of his career or risk forcing his lover to abandon the race. Christopher and Luca face a path more treacherous than any road to the summit.

www.ingramcontent.com/pod-product-compliance
Lightning Source LLC
Chambersburg PA
CBHW020602130626
46552CB00007B/3013